D0938351

EDGE BOOKS™

DRAWING *COOL* STUFF

HOW TO DRAW

GROTESQUE MONSTERS

by Aaron Sautter

illustrated by Brian Bascle

Capstone *press*®

Mankato, Minnesota

Edge Books are published by Capstone Press,
151 Good Counsel Drive, P.O. Box 669, Mankato, Minnesota 56002.
www.capstonepress.com

Library of Congress Cataloging-in-Publication Data
Sautter, Aaron.
How to draw grotesque monsters / by Aaron Sautter; illustrated by Brian Bascle.
p. cm. — (Edge books. Drawing cool stuff)
Includes bibliographical references and index.
Summary: "Lively text and fun illustrations describe how to draw grotesque
monsters" — Provided by publisher.
ISBN–13: 978-1-4296-1300-2 (hardcover)
ISBN–10: 1-4296-1300-9 (hardcover)
1. Monsters in art — Juvenile literature. 2. Drawing — Technique — Juvenile
literature. I. Bascle, Brian. II. Title. III. Series.
NC825.M6S28 2008
743'.87 — dc22   2007025105

Credits
Jason Knudson, set designer; Patrick D. Dentinger, book designer

1 2 3 4 5 6 13 12 11 10 09 08

TABLE OF CONTENTS

WELCOME!

You probably picked this book because you like creepy, gross monsters. Or you picked it because you like to draw. Whatever the reason, get ready to dive into the world of grotesque monsters!

Throughout history, people have made up all sorts of spooky monsters. Creepy vampires, ancient mummies, and big, hairy trolls are all creatures found in our nightmares. But whether they have drooling mouths full of sharp teeth or are hundreds of feet tall, people love being scared by imaginary monsters.

This book is just a starting point. Once you've learned how to draw the different monsters in this book, you can start drawing your own. Let your imagination run wild, and see what sorts of spooky, disgusting monsters you can create!

To get started, you'll need some supplies:

1. First you'll need drawing paper. Any type of blank, unlined paper will do.

2. Pencils are the easiest to use for your drawing projects. Make sure you have plenty of them.

3. You have to keep your pencils sharp to make clean lines. Keep a pencil sharpener close by. You'll use it a lot.

4. As you practice drawing, you'll need a good eraser. Pencil erasers wear out very fast. Get a rubber or kneaded eraser. You'll be glad you did.

5. When your drawing is finished, you can trace over it with a black ink pen or thin felt-tip marker. The dark lines will really make your work stand out.

6. If you decide to color your drawings, colored pencils and markers usually work best. You can also use colored pencils to shade your drawings and make them more lifelike.

One-Eyed Cy

No matter how hard you try, you can't hide from One-Eyed Cy. He's always looking for his next meal. Stay far away from this big cyclops or he might decide to have you for his next dinner!

Try drawing the rest of Cy's body. What do you think his arms and legs look like?

STEP 1

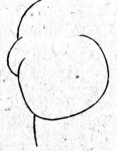

STEP 2

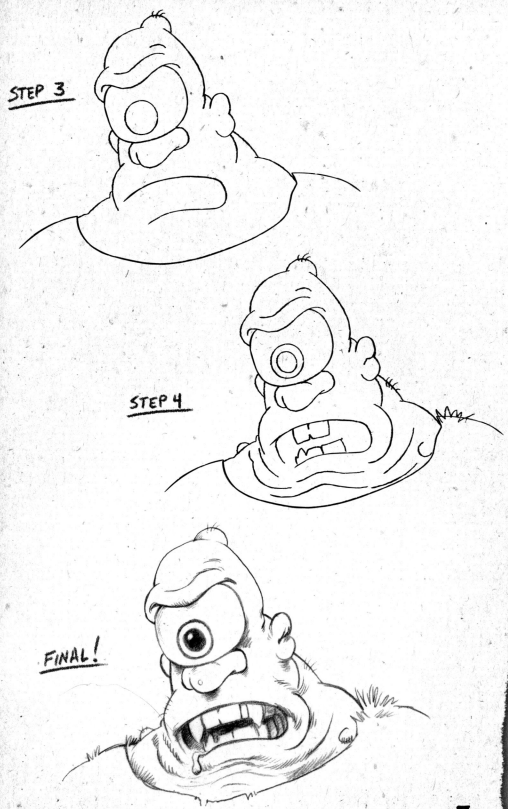

STEP 3

STEP 4

FINAL!

7

COUNT VLAD

Make sure to eat your garlic! Count Vlad hates the stuff. Keep some garlic or holy water around to help chase him away. You definitely don't want to see Vlad hanging around your bedroom window at night!

After drawing Vlad, try drawing him again as a giant vampire bat!

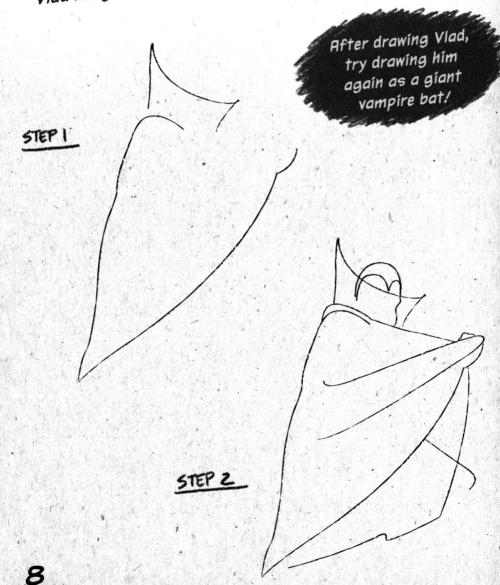

STEP 1

STEP 2

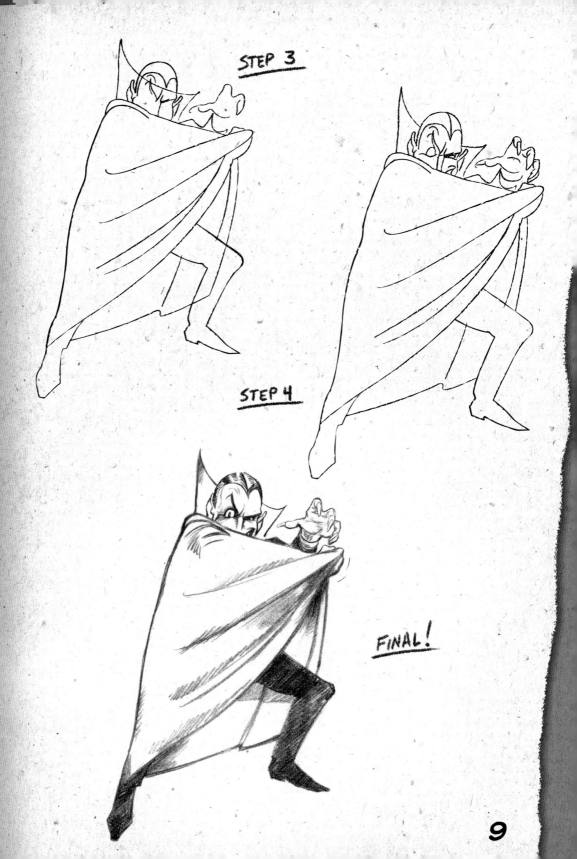

STEP 3

STEP 4

FINAL!

9

KRACKED KARL

Keep away from Kracked Karl the Krazy Klown! He was a simple circus clown who just wanted to make people laugh. But nobody thought he was funny. Now his mission is to make you laugh at his jokes — or else!

After drawing Karl, try giving him a crazy clown suit and some wacky balloons!

STEP 1

STEP 2

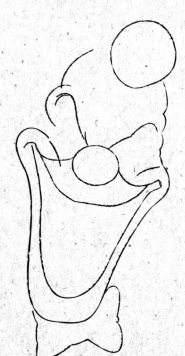

STEP 3

STEP 4

FINAL!

11

MEDUSA

Medusa was once a beautiful woman. All the young men adored her. But the Greek goddess Athena was jealous. She stole Medusa's beauty and changed her hair into hissing snakes. Afterward, any young man who looked at Medusa was turned to stone!

Try drawing Medusa's body. Does she have the body of a normal woman, or of a slippery snake?

STEP 1

STEP 2

STEP 3

STEP 4

FINAL!

13

SKELETAL SOLDIER

Even the bravest warriors tremble in fear when facing an army of Skeletal Soldiers! These undead creatures do not fear death. And they never stop fighting until their bones are smashed to bits.

After practicing this monster, try adding some armor or a bigger shield!

STEP 1

STEP 2

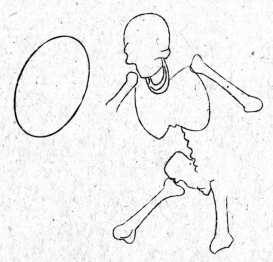

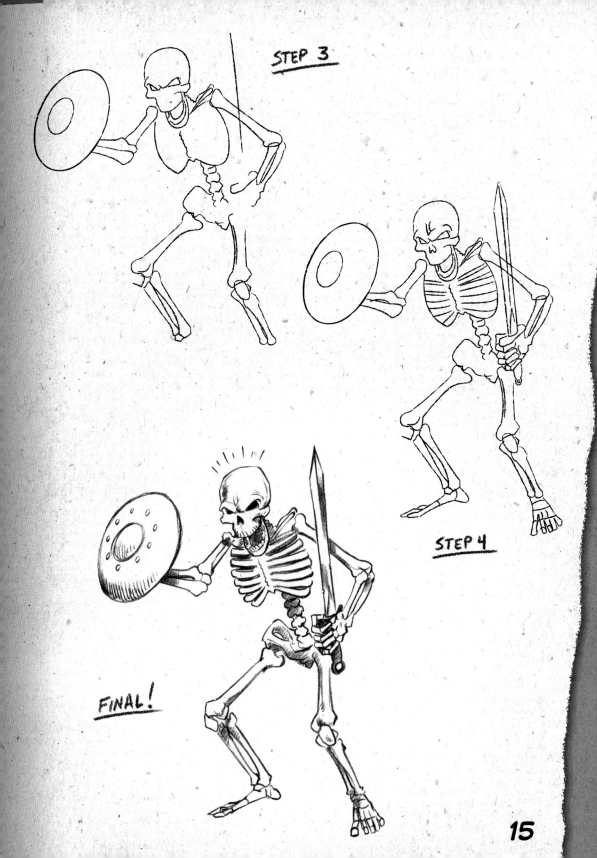

STEP 3

STEP 4

FINAL!

FRANK STEIN

Poor Frank Stein. Nobody understands him. He just wants to be everyone's friend. But people keep chasing him with pitchforks and torches. It's just not easy being 8 feet tall with green skin and bolts sticking out of your head!

After drawing Frank, try drawing him again dancing with his wife!

STEP 1

STEP 2

STEP 3

STEP 4

FINAL!

SINISTER SCARECROW

Don't walk in the fields at night or the Sinister Scarecrow might get you! By day, it's a simple scarecrow stuffed with straw. But by night, it prowls the cornfields looking for its next victim. The crows know to stay away when the sun goes down — and so should you!

After drawing this scary monster, try it again with a pumpkin for a head!

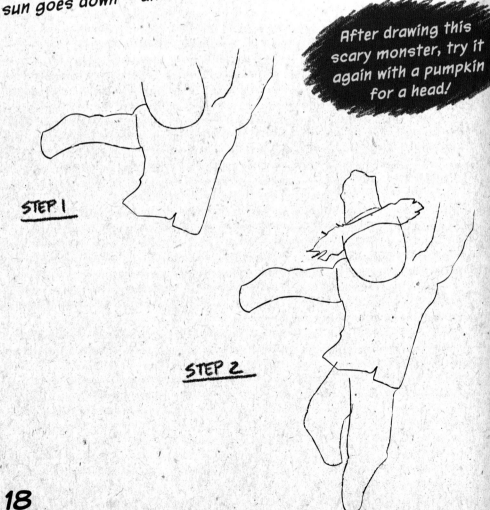

STEP 1

STEP 2

STEP 3

STEP 4

FINAL!

19

KING HOTEP

Who dares to disturb King Hotep's sleep? Watch out, this is one mad mummy! Even after a 3,000-year nap, Hotep still wakes up cranky. Quick, give him a glass of warm milk. Otherwise he might take you on a permanent vacation — to his tomb!

STEP 1

When you're done drawing this mummy, try showing him walking through a museum!

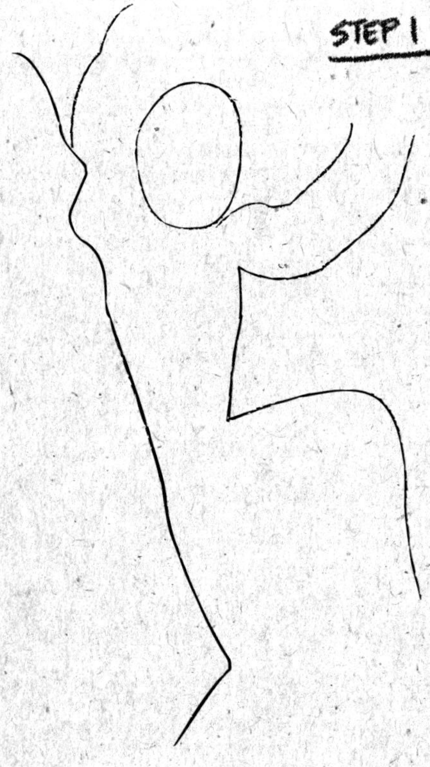

STEP 2

STEP 3

STEP 4

FINAL!

FISHY PHIL

Fishy Phil is a gruesome monster from the deep oceans. His huge eyes help him see in the dark depths. He easily catches prey with his sharp claws. Phil is also an excellent swimmer. You'd better run if you see his scaly head pop out of the water!

After drawing this scaly monster, try showing him catching some fish in the ocean!

STEP 1

STEP 2

STEP 3

STEP 4

FINAL!

23

UGH THE THUG

Ugh is a simple troll. It doesn't take much to make him happy. He loves to catch weary travelers crossing his bridge. Usually, he'll just take all their gold. But sometimes, he'll cook them for his dinner!

Try drawing Ugh in a tug-of-war with his brother Chugh over a bag of stolen gold!

STEP 1

STEP 2

STEP 3

STEP 4

SHIRE
BRIDGE
PAY
ᴿ
TᴼOLL

FINAL!

25

Monster Mash!

Gigantic monsters always seem to be smashing the city of Tokyo, Japan. This time it's King Reptoid versus The Great Ape. Either one could win this brawl. King Reptoid has intense flaming breath, but The Great Ape has superior strength. It's anybody's guess what sorts of giant beasts will show up for Round 2!

After you've mastered this drawing, try it again with your own giant imaginary monsters!

STEP I

STEP 2

STEP 3

TO FINISH THIS DRAWING,
TURN TO THE NEXT PAGE!

STEP 4

STEP 5

STEP 6

FINAL!

GLOSSARY

brawl (BRAWL) — a rough fight

cyclops (SY-klahps) — a giant with one eye in the middle of its forehead

goddess (GOD-iss) — a female supernatural being who is worshipped

grotesque (groh-TESK) — very strange or ugly

holy water (HOH-lee WAW-tur) — water that has been blessed by a priest for religious uses

jealous (JEL-uhss) — wanting something someone else has

pitchfork (PICH-fork) — a large fork with a long handle used for lifting and throwing hay

prey (PRAY) — an animal that is hunted by another animal for food

prowl (PROUL) — to move around quietly and secretly

weary (WIHR-ee) — very tired or exhausted

READ MORE

Barr, Steve. *1-2-3 Draw Cartoon Monsters: A Step-by-Step Guide.* 1-2-3 Draw. Columbus, N.C.: Peel Productions, 2004.

Okum, David. *Draw Super Manga Monsters!* Draw Super! Cincinnati: Impact Books, 2005.

Reinagle, Damon J. *Draw Monsters: A Step-by-Step Guide.* Columbus, N.C.: Peel Productions, 2005.

INTERNET SITES

FactHound offers a safe, fun way to find Internet sites related to this book. All of the sites on FactHound have been researched by our staff.

Here's how:
1. Visit *www.facthound.com*
2. Choose your grade level.
3. Type in this book ID **1429613009** for age-appropriate sites. You may also browse subjects by clicking on letters, or by clicking on pictures and words.
4. Click on the **Fetch It** button.

FactHound will fetch the best sites for you!

INDEX